THE
ELEPHANT'S
GARDEN

THE ELEPHANT'S GARDEN

A traditional Indian folktale
retold and illustrated by

Jane Ray

Boxer Books

In Jasmine's garden there grew the most delicious fruit in the whole village.

There were apples and apricots, kiwis and kumquats, papayas, peaches and passion fruit.

But every night, something was eating the very best fruit.

"Well, we can't have this!"
thought Jasmine.

One night, when everybody else was in bed, she climbed out of her window and hid behind the lotus tree. The hours passed.

The moon rose.

Jasmine kept watch.

CRASH!

An elephant fell from the sky!
He munched all the mangos.
He guzzled all the grapes.
He chomped all the cherries.

"Stop right there, Mr. Elephant!" shouted Jasmine.
"You've eaten all our fruit!"
"I'm very sorry, but I was hungry,"
said the elephant. "And the fruit
here is so delicious. Come with
me and let me show you
my garden."

Jasmine grabbed the elephant's tail and they took off over the treetops. They flew past the moon. They flew past the stars.

They landed on a cloud where another garden grew.
Everything in this garden was . . .

ENORMOUS!

The peaches were as big as soccer balls
and the oranges were the size of ostrich eggs.

The elephant gave Jasmine a gigantic plum.
But it was as hard as glass and impossible
to eat. Every fruit looked delicious,
but was really a precious jewel.
"No wonder you prefer
the fruit in my garden,"
said Jasmine.

At sunset the elephant was hungry again.
He offered Jasmine one ruby strawberry to
show her mom, and they flew back home.

Jasmine's family were very worried
about her. But they could hardly
believe it when she showed them
the great big ruby strawberry and told
them about the elephant's garden.
They wanted to see it for themselves.

"I'll take you tonight," promised Jasmine, "but you mustn't tell anyone or they'll all want to come."

But Little Hassan saw his friend Kali.
"It can't hurt to tell Kali,"
thought Hassan. "After all,
she is my best friend . . . "

Who told Aunty Sita and Uncle Deepak.
Before long everybody had heard
about the precious jewels in
the elephant's garden.

Kali went straight home and told her mom. Who told her cousin Bakool.

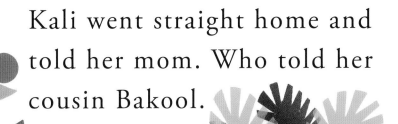

"If we can have some of those jewels for ourselves we will be rich!" they said.

When the moon rose, there they all were,
wanting to visit the elephant's garden.
They hid in the bushes and waited, until –

CRASH –

the elephant landed by the
mango tree.

When he was full the elephant flew up into the night sky with everyone holding hands and trailing after him.

When they reached the stars Cousin Bakool called to Aunty Sita, "Tell me again – how big are those oranges?"

Aunty Sita couldn't remember so she asked Kali, who asked Little Hassan.

"Jasmine," called Little Hassan, "how big did you say the oranges are?"

"Wait and see," said Jasmine.

"We'll be there soon."

But Cousin Bakool couldn't wait.

"Tell us now," he said.

"They are as big as ostrich eggs," said Jasmine.

Cousin Bakool had never seen an ostrich egg.

"How big is that?" he called up from the
bottom of the line.

Exasperated, Jasmine shouted,

"They are this big!" and she held
out both her hands . . .

And she and Little Hassan, Kali and Aunty Sita, Cousin Bakool and all the other friends and relations, tumbled back down to earth and landed with a wallop by the mango tree.

The elephant never came back.
He must have found somewhere
more peaceful to eat his dinner.

So Jasmine's family and friends
never did visit the elephant's
garden after all.
But they did get to eat the
delectable dates and plump
apricots, the sweet strawberries
and luscious lychees in
Jasmine's beautiful garden.

For Maureen Hanscomb
Jane Ray

First American edition published in 2017
by Boxer Books Limited.

Distributed in the United States and Canada by
Sterling Publishing Co., Inc.
1166 Avenue of the Americas, New York, New York 10036

First published in Great Britain in 2017
by Boxer Books Limited.
www.boxerbooks.com

The illustrations were prepared using cut-paper collage and paint.

The text is set in Adobe Garamond Pro

ISBN 978-1-910716-22-9
1 3 5 7 9 10 8 6 4 2

Printed in China

All of our papers are sourced from managed forests and renewable resources.